say something

BY PEGGY MOSS / ILLUSTRATED BY LEA LYON

"If you think you are too small to make a difference,
try sleeping in a room with a mosquito." African Proverb

TILBURY HOUSE
PUBLISHERS

THOMASTON, MAINE

There's a kid in my school who gets picked on all the time.

I think he's sad.

I think he's sad because he keeps his head down
when he walks down the hall—

—and he hardly ever says hello.

I don't pick on him.

I feel sorry for him.

There's another kid in my school who gets teased.

He gets called names.

When he's moving through the halls, kids push him
and tell him he's slow.

I walk on the other side of the hall.
I don't say those things.

A girl who rides on my bus
always sits alone.

Sometimes kids throw things at her and call her names.

The girls who sit behind her laugh.

I don't laugh.

I don't say anything.

One day my friends were out, and I had to sit

alone in the cafeteria.

Some kids came over to me and they started telling jokes.

I laughed until the jokes started to be about me.

My face burned. I looked down at the table.

I sat on my hands to keep them from moving so much.

I tried not to cry, but it was hard not to cry,

and when they saw my face getting wet,

the kids started laughing.

I wished I could stop crying.

I wished I could disappear.

When the kids left, I looked around the cafeteria.

I was surprised to see that the cafeteria was full of students.

There were even kids I knew, sitting at the table

right next to mine.

They were looking at me.
I could tell they
felt sorry for me.

When I went home, I told my big brother
I was mad at the kids at the table next to mine.

He shrugged and said, "Why? They didn't do anything."
"Right," I said.

On the bus the next day,
I sat next to the girl who
always sits alone.

She's really funny!

Author Peggy Moss
Says Something!

I wrote *Say Something* after meeting a young woman who had been teased relentlessly in high school, with terrible consequences. Nobody spoke up for her. Not once. "Sarah" was almost thirty when we met and was training to become a school nurse. She had just run into a former classmate who had said, "I always wanted to tell you I felt sorry for you in high school." As if that was enough. As if Sarah should be grateful that someone who had watched her become miserable and isolated felt bad about it.

I literally ran back to my office after meeting Sarah and wrote down the words that became *Say Something*. I could never have imagined the journey that ensued! The kids I've worked with have taught me hundreds of different ways to speak up and zillions of ways to be brave and resilient. This 10th-anniversary edition is dedicated to the kids I've met and the kids I'll meet in the future—because you amaze me! You have reminded me that it's hard to speak up—for yourself or for somebody else. You've talked about how complicated cyber teasing can be. And you've discovered that speaking up can be thankless, but you speak up anyway—in your own, uniquely-you ways. Because of you, those of us who get teased feel less alone and better able to speak up for ourselves.

Do you think
YOU can make a difference?

Say something! **Like what?**

Students everywhere are stepping up to say, "That's not cool!" when other kids bully in school. And their words are making a world of difference. Choose your own way to say, "I don't want to hear that!"
Then, practice, practice, practice!
Keep your goal in mind: make the teasing stop! Remember, humor works, but teasing back does not.

When you see someone else being teased, **try these:**

• Say something to the person who is getting teased. It doesn't matter what you say, really. Just saying "Hi" to someone you don't usually hang out with works. So does, "Come play on our team." Or, "Can I sit with you at lunch today?"

• Say something to the bully. Don't become part of the fight. But remember, often just a quick word or two will make the teasing or the mean-spirited joke stop. Every one of us has our own way of saying, "I don't want to hear that." Try: "Knock it off...." "Cut it out...." "That's so ten minutes ago!" "Oh, nice one." Or, "Yeah, that's cool." Or, "Grow up."

• Tell an adult—a parent, teacher, principal, school nurse, or someone else you trust. When teasing changes to pushing or feels scary, it's important for you to let someone know, before anyone gets hurt.

Why **speak up?**

• Because you can make teasing UN-cool. Most bullies tease because they want YOU to think they are cool. But teasing isn't cool. It's mean. If you don't laugh when a bully makes a joke about another kid, the joke is over. And when that happens, you've made a huge difference.

• If you don't, who will? When no one steps up to stop the teasing, the bullies get bolder, and often someone gets hurt.

• Because teasing will happen to you. (It happens to all of us.) You're going to want someone to speak up for you. So—show them how it's done.

YOU can *!*

If you are being bullied, speak up!

Things to say are: "Please stop." "That hurts my feelings." "I haven't done anything to you." Don't be afraid to tell an adult!

Want to find out more?

Check out these organizations and their websites:

• Partners Against Hate
This organization offers promising education and counterracism strategies for youth and community professionals to fight prejudice and bigotry.
www.Partnersagainsthate.org

• The Giraffe Project
If you want inspiration about people with the courage to stick their necks out for the common good, visit this site. www.giraffe.org

• Kids' Quest
This site will help you understand more about kids with health problems or disabilities. www.cdc.gov/ncbddd/kids

• PREVnet
This is a national network of leading researchers and organizations, working together to stop bullying in Canada. www.prevnet.ca

Want to do more?

• Bring a speaker to your school.

• Start a school anti-bullying campaign. There are many new and different programs being developed for school-based approaches. A good place to start is Don't Laugh at Me. Originally a song and then a book by Steve Seskin and now a program run by Peter Yarrow of Peter, Paul, and Mary fame, Operation Respect is free and has been used in thousands of schools. www.operationrespect.org

Remember YOU are the very best person to bring a change to your school.

Since its release in May 2004, this book has sparked "Say Something" weeks in schools from Maine to Shanghai. It has been turned into plays, distributed to hundreds of kids at conferences, read by principals on large screens, and rewritten by students in several schools (*Do Something!* is a favorite title). Most importantly, *Say Something* has helped start countless conversations among kids and adults about teasing.

Say Something has given me the extraordinary pleasure of talking to thousands of kids all over North America and meeting a wide range of adults—school counselors, teachers, nurses, and parents—who keep a copy of *Say Something* nearby, talk about it, and loan it out. You caring adults are the backup these incredible kids need and deserve, and I am grateful to you every day.

As *Say Something* turns 10 and meets new, courageous kids determined to feel safe at school and adults committed to helping them, I remind you to speak up. You will make a difference. You *do* make a difference.

Thank you!
Peggy Moss
Toronto, July 2013

TILBURY HOUSE, PUBLISHERS
12 Starr Street, Thomaston, Maine 04861
800-582-1899 • www.tilburyhouse.com

First hardcover printing: May 2004 • 10 9 8 7
First 10th-anniversary paperback printing: October 2013 • 10 9 8 7 6 5

Dedications
For the kids who get teased, because you are not alone. And for the kids who speak up, because you make all the difference. And for Teddy. —PM
For Joni, Carlie, and Bernie —LL

Acknowledgments
Thank you to Steve Wessler for the chance, Betsy Sweet for the nudge, and Audrey, Jennifer, and Lea for giving the words life. Thanks to Paula and Ted Moss, who taught us to speak up. And thank you, John Beebe, for everything. —PM

My thanks to Ms. Jensen's seventh-grade class at John Muir Middle School in San Leandro, California, Mr. Chapnick's fifth-grade class at Lorin Eden School in Hayward, California, the fifth-grade summer day camp group at the Richmond YMCA in California, and, especially, Cameron, my narrator. I couldn't have illustrated this book without you. —LL

Library of Congress Cataloging-in-Publication Data

Moss, Peggy, 1966-
   Say something / Peggy Moss ; illustrated by Lea Lyon. — 10th anniversary edition.
      pages cm
   Summary: A child who never says anything when other children are being teased or bullied finds herself in their position one day when jokes are made at her expense and no one speaks up.
   ISBN 978-0-88448-364-9 (hardcover : alk. paper) — ISBN 978-0-88448-360-1 (pbk. : alk. paper)
   [1. Bullying—Fiction. 2. Assertiveness (Psychology)—Fiction. 3. Schools—Fiction.]
I. Lyon, Lea, 1945- illustrator. II. Title.
   PZ7.M85357Say 2014
   [E]—dc23   2013027583

Printed by Pacom, Inc.,Kyunggi-do, Korea